Weekly Reader Children's Book Club presents

TRIXIE,
THE
HALLOWEEN PUPPY

by Marilyn Sapienza

Illustrations by Jane Demelis

Weekly Reader Books, Middletown, Connecticut

Cover and text illustrations by Jane Demelis.
Book design by C. Angela Mohr.

In the shuttered house on the corner lived the Hart family. And with them lived their shaggy puppy, Trixie. Trixie had floppy ears, a wig-wag tail, and a wet nose.

Trixie was an ordinary puppy. She liked to sit up and roll over. She liked to chase her tail and chew Daddy's slippers. Trixie was usually a happy puppy. But sometimes she got lonely.

October 31st was one of those lonely days for Trixie. Everyone seemed too busy for her. Grammy was roasting pumpkin seeds in the kitchen. Daddy and Dottie were carving a jack-o-lantern in the dining room. And Mother and Danny were working on a Halloween costume in the living room.

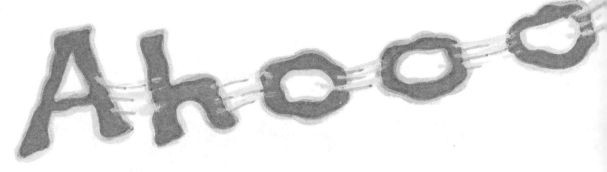

Trixie sat in her doggie bed. She called to everyone with a sad howl: "Ahoooo. Ahoooo." She waited. But nobody came.

Trixie jumped out of her bed and went to the kitchen. She stood in the doorway and waited. Grammy didn't seem to notice her. Grammy went right on reading from her cookbook. "Sprinkle one cup of crushed pumpkin seeds into the batter," Grammy read out loud.

Trixie perked up her ears when she heard Grammy say *seeds*. She looked around. She saw a tray on the counter. There were lots of tiny toasted things on it. They smelled so good. The yummy smell made Trixie's nose go twitch-twitch-twitch. Trixie jumped up on the kitchen chair and dove head-first onto the tray. The seeds went flying this way and that way. They scattered here, there, and everywhere!

"Oh, no!" yelled Grammy. "How could you, Trixie? Look at the mess you've made! Go away!" Poor Trixie! She only wanted to see what Grammy was making.

Trixie went into the dining room. She stood
in the doorway and waited. But Daddy and Dottie
didn't seem to notice her. "Daddy," said Dottie,
"give the pumpkin head a scary-looking face."
Trixie perked up her ears when
she heard Dottie say
pumpkin head.

She looked around. She saw a pumpkin head on the table. It looked horrible. It looked frightening. "Grrrr," growled Trixie. "Grrruf, grrruf."

"Oh, Trixie," scolded Daddy. "Stop making all that noise. You're hurting my ears. Go away!" Poor Trixie! She was only trying to protect Daddy and Dottie from the horrible pumpkin head.

Grrruf

Trixie went into the living room. She stood in the doorway and waited. But Mother and Danny didn't seem to notice her. "Stand still, Danny," said Mother. "I want to see how much cloth I need for your costume." Trixie perked up her ears when she heard Mother say *cloth*.

She looked around and saw a pile of material on the floor. Trixie took one end in her mouth and ran around and around.

"Stop, Trixie, stop!" shouted Mother. "Put that down! You're ruining everything!" Poor Trixie! She was only trying to help.

Suddenly, everyone was standing in the room, looking at Trixie. *No, no, no* went Grammy's head. "Trixie is a nuisance," she said. *Tap, tap, tap* went Daddy's foot. "Trixie is a pest," he said.

Shake, shake, shake went Mother's finger. "Trixie is a problem," she said.

Trixie knew she had been naughty. Her ears drooped. Her head hung low. Her tail didn't go wig-wag.

Then Danny said in a quiet voice, "I think Trixie is just feeling left out. Everyone's been so busy with Halloween plans that we've ignored Trixie."

Dottie knelt down beside Trixie and patted her head. "I'm sorry. We haven't been paying any attention to you." She paused for a minute. "And now that I'm taking a good look at you, Trixie, you remind me of Halloween."

"What do you mean?" asked Daddy.

"Well," said Dottie. "Trixie is as white as a
Halloween ghost. And her nose is as black as a
witch's hat." Trixie tilted her head to the right.
Her left ear lifted just a little.

"That's right," said Danny. "Trixie, your eyes are as round as a Halloween moon. And your tongue is as bright as a Halloween pumpkin." Trixie tilted her head to the left. Her tail went thump-thump.

Grammy chuckled. "And when you thump your tail like that, Trixie, you sound like the house shutters that bang in the Halloween wind."

Mother smiled. "Trixie, sometimes you're as sweet as the Halloween treats the children collect." Trixie let out a happy howl. "Ahoooo. Ahoooo."

"And your howl reminds me of Halloween sounds at midnight," said Daddy, covering his ears.

"Even your name sounds like what we say on Halloween," said Dottie. "Trick or treat!" Trixie bounced up and down, up and down.

"I'm glad Trixie is feeling like part of the family again," said Mother. "But what am I going to do with the cloth that she tore?"

"Can't we use it for Trixie?" asked Danny. "We can make her a costume so that she can go trick-or-treating with us tonight."

"Well, OK," said Mother. "But I'll need some help."

Together, the Hart family planned Trixie's costume.

Mother cut the cloth into a long rectangle.
Grammy sewed lots of lace to the strip of cloth.
Dottie threaded a needle and pushed it in and
out of the material.

Danny carefully pulled it and
gathered it into a ruffle.

The children tied the ruffle around Trixie's neck. Then Daddy found an old hat with a funny pom-pom at the top. He put it on Trixie's head. Trixie sat patiently while the family dressed her for Halloween.

"There," said Grammy. "Now you look like the funny clown that you are." Trixie perked up her ears when she heard Grammy say *clown*.

She looked around. She saw everyone watching her. So Trixie sat up.

She rolled over. She chased her tail.
Everyone laughed.

At last, Trixie was a happy puppy
because *now* she was the Harts' Halloween
puppy.